370382452

D0548211

Pie Corbett

SPEAK OUT!

Great ideas for speaking and listening activities for ages 9-11

Illustrations by Helen James

A&C Black • London

First published in 2006 by
A & C Black Publishers Ltd
38 Soho Square, London WID 3HB

www.acblack.com

Designed and illustrated by Helen James
Edited by Mary-Jane Wilkins

ISBN   Hardback 9-780-7136-7222-0
        Paperback 9-780-7136-7223-7

A CIP record for this book is available from
the British Library.

A & C Black uses paper produced with elemental
chlorine-free pulp, harvested from managed
sustainable forests.

Printed in Great Britain by CPD Wales.

Contents

1

Voices round the world

We're at it all the time – talking. It's going on right now across the world – millions of voices, all talking. It's one of the most important things that we do. If you don't believe me, just look at some of the words we use for different kinds of speaking (right).

When you talk, you can make people laugh or cry. You can end a war or start one. Talking is important – but strangely enough, it is not something anyone ever teaches you. You're just supposed to be good at it.

So how good are you at talking? Have you ever felt tongue-tied? Have you ever stumbled over your words, not quite able to explain what you wanted to say? How would you manage if you had to make a presentation to the school?

This book is all about becoming good at talking – and its best friend – listening. If you are not good at listening, all sorts of problems can arise – if you want to catch a train to Southampton and don't listen carefully to the announcements, you could end up on a train to Southend instead!

This first chapter gives you some background to the whole tricky business of speaking.

tittle tattle bawl lisp talk argue
bellow prattle intone blether grass
burble call out refute chatter
screech chin-wag clamour mutter
converse declaim let on discuss
exclaim squeal gas blurt out
stutter croak rasp scream harp on
allude to speak complain inform jaw
jibe gabble
lament mention
natter drawl
tell rant
object jeer orate
drivel on plead yell
mumble blab preach
howl whisper rave
spout recite gossip relate roar groan
witter on cry say shout confess
shriek whinge grunt declare
murmur slur comment drone assert
snap jabber spill the beans moan
splutter gibber tell tales
pronounce titter harangue wail
rabbit stammer whine yatter
whimper babble

When do we speak and

We spend most of our lives speaking
or listening – we do it all the time.

- Acting on stage.

- Broadcasting on radio.

- Debating ideas in School Council.

- Planning a trip.

- Chatting over meals.

- Telling a story.

- Congratulating someone.

- Listening to CDs or podcasts.

- Writing a shopping list together.

- Performing in class assemblies.

- Investigating a science problem.

What are speaking and listening skills?

Speaking skills
- Speaking clearly.
- Being loud enough to be heard.
- Looking at the person you are speaking to.
- Varying your expression.
- Not talking too quickly.
- Taking turns.
- Thinking before speaking.
- Adjusting what you say according to who you are talking to and why.
- Letting others contribute.
- Being prepared to change your ideas.
- Changing how you speak to suit the audience and situation.
- Avoiding repeating yourself.
- Remembering people's feelings.

Listening skills

- Smiling and responding.
- Looking at the speaker.
- Clarifying by recapping.
- Asking questions if you don't understand.
- Nodding and making eye contact.
- Making encouraging noises.
- Recalling the main ideas.
- Replying to what has been said.
- Being aware of the speaker's feelings.
- Remembering the main points made.
- Asking questions to show interest.

Listening to good talkers

If you want to be good at talking, listen to some of the best speakers to see how they do it! Try listening to storytellers, poets, politicians speaking in the Houses of Parliament, film stars acting, comedians telling jokes, pop singers performing, TV soap stars, radio and TV reporters, newsreaders and weather forecasters.

Class rules

When you have about 30 people in a classroom, it becomes very noisy if everyone talks at once. What rules do you have for class talk?

Rules for talking

- Take turns.
- Put up your hand and wait till you are asked to speak.
- Keep your comments relevant to the topic.
- Be ready to ask people to explain ideas further.
- Build on other people's ideas.
- Propose new ideas if you are getting stuck.
- Respect ideas you don't agree with.
- Try to add more points to a discussion.
- Support what you say by giving reasons.
- Keep to the point (try not to ramble).
- Use gestures to make what you say sound interesting.
- Don't make unkind remarks – remember how your audience might feel.
- Be ready to change your mind if you hear a good idea
- Think before you speak: what might be interesting or useful to say?

Rules for listening

- Remember the main points of what is being said.
- Keep notes of information or ideas that you might forget.
- Show by your expression that you are interested.
- Wait your turn to speak.
- Don't interrupt.
- Don't giggle or fidget while someone is speaking – it can be off-putting.
- Look at the speaker and try to follow what is being said.
- Ask about anything you don't understand or that needs more information or explanation.
- Listen to what is being said rather than thinking about what you want to say.
- Comment on what has been said or add another idea.

Working in a group

Working in a group can be a disaster! Have you ever had to work with someone who talks all the time and doesn't listen? And what about people who are only interested in their own ideas – they don't make good group members.

How to set about group work
- Be clear about the task you have been set – what do you have to do?
- Make a note of how long you have.
- Decide how to tackle the task – all together or splitting into pairs for a while and then coming back together.
- Create a timetable, noting what has to be done and by when.
- Agree to review how you are doing five minutes before the deadline.

What do you say if you disagree?
Working with a partner or in a group when you disagree with what is being suggested can be difficult. How can you put forward your ideas without upsetting someone? Here are some suggestions for comments you could make:

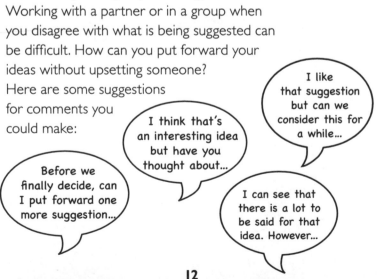

I like that suggestion but can we consider this for a while...

I think that's an interesting idea but have you thought about...

Before we finally decide, can I put forward one more suggestion...

I can see that there is a lot to be said for that idea. However...

Group roles

Choose people to play different roles in the group.
Try to make sure each person is suited to their role.

Chairperson
Organizes and runs the group. The chair's job is
to make sure that the group completes the task.

Scribe
Writes down any ideas or decisions. The scribe needs
to be able to write quickly and clearly and should reread
what has been written before feeding back to the class.

Reporter
Works with the scribe and gives feedback, reporting
from the group to the class. The reporter needs to be
confident and have a clear voice. It is their job to list the
group's ideas on a poster or an interactive whiteboard
for everyone to see. The reporter should be ready to
explain the thinking behind the ideas.

Mentor
Helps to get the job done. The mentor should make
sure everyone has a chance to contribute. This means
asking each group member whether they have anything
extra to add or say every now and then. The mentor
should check that everyone agrees with decisions.

Timekeeper
Watches the clock to make sure the group finishes on
time. This person has the important job of making sure
the group concentrates and does not waste time.

2
Giving a talk

You may be asked to give a talk in school or to work in a group to prepare a presentation. This might be about some work you have been doing in class. In real life there are all sorts of situations where you might need this skill.

Giving a business presentation

Selling produce in a market

Organizing a mountain rescue

How to set about giving a talk

Your audience

Your audience matters. You must interest them or they'll soon doze off – so think of ways to grab their attention. Good attention grabbers include telling jokes, using pictures, showing a video clip, putting up posters, using objects or documents, staging short role plays and involving the listeners. What you say and how you say it depends on your audience.

Your purpose and message

Think carefully about why you are giving the talk – what do the listeners need to get out of it? Are you trying to give them some information or explain how to do something? By the end of the talk your listeners should have received your message. This involves careful planning.

Planning

Planning a talk involves four stages.

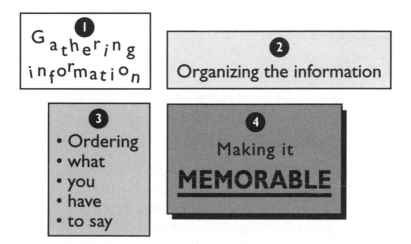

1. Gathering information

2. Organizing the information

3.
• Ordering
• what
• you
• have
• to say

4. Making it MEMORABLE

Top tips for gathering information

Begin planning by making a simple chart. In the first
column list what you know about the topic. Then write
a list of questions – what else do you need to know?
Leave the third column blank to write in the answers.

What we know	What we want to find out	New information
Second World War started in 1939	Why did it start?	
Winston Churchill was prime minister	What did he do? Where did he live?	
George VI was king	Did he leave	
Children were evacuated	Why?	

Where will you look for information? If you were giving
a presentation about life in the Second World War, you
might try these sources:

*information books   encyclopaedias   museums
the library   the Internet   CD-ROMs
experts on the subject (interview them)
places which were important during the war*

Organizing your information

Once you have gathered all sorts of information, you need to think about timing. How long will your talk last? Sort your information and get rid of what doesn't matter. Think about which pieces are essential.

Put the information into a clear diagram. Here are three ways to organize information. Make sure you think about the order – what should be said first (introduction), what in the middle (main content) and what at the end (final points).

1 A flow chart

Write information and key points inside the boxes.

1 September 1939
All men between 18 and 40
had to join up.

By 1941 more men were needed
so men aged up to 51 had to join.

Single women aged 20 to 30
had to do war work – working
in factories or on the land.

2 A time line

This is helpful for showing an order over time, such as the details of someone's life or a sequence of events.

1919
End of First World War

3 September 1939
Second World War begins

May/June 1939
Dunkirk landing

September 1939
Evacuation of children starts

June 1940
Battle of Britain

1940-41
The Blitz

1941
The Japanese bomb Pearl Harbor
The USA joins the war

1944
The Allies land in Normandy

7 May 1945
War ends

3   A web

Write the main heading in the centre.

Ways to grab attention

We've all sat through dull talks and presentations. How can you give your audience information in an interesting way? Here are some top tips.

Make it visual
- Bring in objects, e.g. a gas mask.
- Use real documents, e.g. a ration book.
- Demonstrate something, e.g. how to put on a gas mask.
- Dress up, e.g. as an air raid warden.
- Show diagrams, posters, photos or illustrations.
- Use the OHP, interactive whiteboard or a computer.
- Show a short video clip.
- Use cards with key points or words written large.

Use action
- Use role play, e.g. interview a child about being an evacuee.
- Act out a scene, e.g. Churchill and the king on the balcony.
- Pull ideas out of a hat as if you were a conjuror.
- Pull cards from a fact box.
- Pin up key points on a board.
- Use a puppet to make key points.
- Pause for a buzz – allow 30 seconds for the audience to talk about a point just made.

Include sounds
- Play sound effects, e.g. bombs falling and exploding.
- Play a short snatch of music or a song, e.g. Vera Lynn singing 'The White Cliffs of Dover' or 'We'll Meet Again'.

- Chant a poem, e.g. 'Dulce Et Decorum Est' by Wilfred Owen.
- Sing a song, e.g. 'It's a Long Way to Tipperary'.
- Play a speech recording, e.g. one of Churchill's speeches.

Make it fun
- Use a 'did you know', e.g. Did you know that a gas mask was called a Mickey Mouse because it was red and black and looked a bit like the cartoon of Mickey Mouse?
- Play 'true or false', e.g. Is it true that there were no pips in raspberry jam but there were little chips of wood instead?
- Play a game.
- Ask the audience to vote or decide on an issue.
- Use jokes where appropriate.

Beware!
If too much is happening then the audience might be distracted, so decide on just a few ideas for making the information interesting and memorable.

Did you know that you forget most of what you hear – but if you see information, listen to it and talk about it you are more likely to remember it? Make sure you use visual and active ideas.

Formal or informal?

Whether you are formal or informal depends on your audience. If you are presenting ideas at an assembly, you will need to be formal.
If you are sharing your findings within a small group, you could use more informal language.

Practise!

Once you have gathered and sorted the information, worked out the length and thought of some attention grabbers, practise. This is important.

Groups need to decide who starts, who says what and who finishes. The opening is important and so is the ending. End on the most important point, then repeat your main ideas.

Find somewhere quiet to practise. Pretend you have an audience and go over exactly what you are going to say and do. It helps if someone checks the time.

If you can, record or video yourselves so that you can hear /see what the presentation looks like.

Most people use notes to help them. Keep them on postcards – don't write down everything, just list the main points.

Giving the talk

When the day arrives what really matters is sticking to the plan. There are a few key things to bear in mind.

Volume is the most important. Your audience must be able to hear what you say, so do not speak too softly. Make sure you practise this again and again. Stand up straight and look towards the back of the room. Push out your voice so that it bounces off the back wall.

Pace is also important. If you talk too fast the audience will not be able to grasp your points. Make sure you don't gabble.

Clarity is crucial. Make sure you speak clearly. If you mumble or are indistinct, your audience will start muttering, 'What was that?' Avoid rambling or leaving too many gaps, or saying 'um' or 'er' too often. Try to be clear.

> Anti-nerves tactic:
> stop feeling nervous by
> breathing deeply a few times.

Look round the room. If you scan the room as you are talking the audience will feel you are talking to them – so they are more likely to listen.

Draw in the audience – this means talking to them. Ask questions: 'Have you ever wondered why…?' or say: 'Now you can see…' Use the word 'you' and try to sound friendly!

Keep to the plan. Use your postcard notes – and do not be tempted to add other ideas or you could overrun.

When others are making presentations, think about what makes them successful – what tricks did they use that you could try? Or think about why it wasn't good – what should you avoid? The most common reason a presentation is unsuccessful is that no one can hear!

3

Persuading people

We use all sorts of tricks to persuade people to go along with our views and ideas. Some of the best persuaders are politicians, but the champions at this are the people who make advertisements. They have to persuade us to buy what they are selling. TV ads have just a few seconds to make an impact, so every word is chosen carefully.

Mum cooks it for a only few minutes at home...

Persuading the cook not to overcook the cabbage.

Radio broadcast persuading people to eat more healthily.

Remember your five portions of fruit and vegetables every day...

Persuading someone to buy a pet.

Persuading people to buy a particular product.

Persuading a child to come down to safety.

Persuasive tricks

Try watching some ads to spot the tricks advertisers use. One thing you will notice is that different ads are aimed at different audiences – some aim to sell to children, some to teenagers, some to mums, some to dads and some to people with different interests. Can you spot the various tricks used to sell to different people?

Advertising techniques

Visual tricks
Images that make the product look good.

Music and voices
The right music can make a car seem fast and exciting – or a sofa comfy and restful. Advertisers also think about the type and tone of voice they use for the voiceover. For teenagers, they might choose a loud, fast-talking person to give street cred. Ads for older people are more likely to use a traditional accent, and a mellow, comforting voice.

Cool
Actors who look cool are shown with the product to make you feel that you will become a cool person if you buy it.

Famous people
Advertisers often pay well-known faces to promote products so you feel, 'Well, if it's OK for them then it will be OK for me.'

Free offers
Advertisers like to seem generous, and prepared to give you something for nothing.

Implying something
Through this technique, the advertiser makes it seem that you might be left behind or suffer if you do not buy their product.

Portraying benefits
Advertisers show happy, healthy looking people using their products to suggest that you too will be like them – if you buy!

The right colours
Action toys are often shown in bright colours to make them seem exciting.

Shocking pictures
Sometimes images of something horrific can be persuasive. People trying to raise money for a charity might use this tactic.

Before and after pictures
The ad shows someone before using a product looking rather weary, old and depressed, and then 'only six weeks later' a picture of the same person looking cheery and fit.

How words persuade

How does an advertiser persuade you to spend your pocket money on the latest toy or gadget in only half a minute? Here are some tricks.

Questions
These engage the listener and make them listen. They make it sound as though the ad is speaking directly to you:
Have you ever wondered...
Feeling unhappy? If so, you need...

Lists of facts and statistics
These are used to prove a product is scientific or has been shown to work.

Alliteration
Repeating sounds at the start of words close to each other. The repeated B sound in **B**uy **B**ritish **B**urgers makes the line memorable.

Rhyme
Rhyme is used for the same reason – catchy phrases and jingles stay in people's minds:
At Mills you get thrills and spills!

Repetition
An advertiser has only a few seconds to make sure the listener gets the point and remembers the product. This means that the name of the product is often repeated.

Imperatives

These are orders - and advertisers use them to persuade us to buy their product:

Buy now!
Call us now!
Make sure you have a...
Only eat Mister Muffins!

Boastful words

Most advertising uses a few powerful words to persuade you that a particular product is the best. A car might be:

a dream on wheels or **supercharged**.

Films are usually:

action-packed and **unmissable**.

Advertisers choose words to boast about their product.

Patterns of three

Repeating something three times comes from storytelling (three bears, three billy goats). Advertisers use it to hammer home their points:

The brightest, the boldest and the best in town...

Short sentences

Advertisers use short sentences for dramatic impact:

Laze about by sheltered lagoons. Treat yourself.
Stay in luxury. Stay at Calming Hotel.

Up-to-the-minute language

This is used for selling to young people. Even spelling:

TXT US 2 C!

Persuading people to your view

When you are planning to persuade someone to see something from your point of view, you have to think about two important things: the advantages and the disadvantages.

Advantages
Make it clear what they will gain by agreeing with your point of view.

Disadvantages or worries
What might stop them from agreeing? Do you have answers to their concerns (they are called counter-arguments)? It's worth having some responses ready!

The key to persuasion is to think about the people you are trying to persuade and why you are trying to persuade them. Think about the points you want to make, then put them in the most effective order. Provide evidence and reasons to back up what you are saying. Defend and explain your views.

Selling the zoo park
Imagine you've been hired to persuade a small village to sell their land for a zoo park. There is a meeting with the villagers and you have two minutes to persuade them that this is a good idea. What tricks might you use? Put yourself in their shoes – what might they be concerned about? Make some notes and try to think of useful answers.

Villagers' worries	Possible answers
Wild animals might escape	High electric fences
The park will look ugly	Screening with trees
Noise	Earth mounds will dull noise
Lots of tourists	Numbers will be limited
More traffic	New/wider roads to be built
Parking	A new car park

Now list the advantages that might persuade them to agree.

Advantages for the village
- Free membership all year round for villagers and their families.
- Job opportunities.
- More customers for village shop, pub, garage, etc.
- Improved local road system.
- Annual gift from zoo to village hall of £1,000.
- Opening by a famous personality – villagers invited.
- Adults in village can join zoo social club.
- Free visit every year for village school.
- Good price for the land – above its value.

Now think about what might encourage the villagers to agree to sell the land for a zoo. Here are some ideas.

Sound friendly
Try to make the villagers feel that you are a kind person (someone like them) who has their best interests at heart: 'I was brought up in a village and like you I value a quiet life so we have designed the zoo so that all noise will be cut out...'

Appeal to their better feelings
'I know that many of you are interested in saving wildlife and will be pleased to join our project to save the rare wild ebu...'

Ask questions
'Do the kids get bored at weekends?'
'Would you like a part-time job that pays well?'

Give appealing facts
For example, explain that the extra large car park will hold up to 1,000 cars.

Use powerful words

One of the best-kept zoos in the world.

The world's wildest and most extraordinary creatures right on your doorstep...

An amazing opportunity not to be missed...

The presentation will need visual support – the villagers might want to see what the zoo will look like, where the roads and car park will be and how the noise will be reduced by the fencing and earth mounds. You could show photos of people working, children visiting and some of the amazing animals.

Holding a class debate

Debates use persuasive tricks, but differ from presentations because during a debate people argue both sides of a viewpoint. Debates are built around topics about which there may be strongly held opinions – such as whether the school should build a skateboard ramp on the playground.

Preparing for a class debate

1 First you need a topic that people feel strongly about – one about which people have different views.

2 You then need the following people:
> • A person to introduce the topic and teams
> • A small team who agree with the topic
> • A small team who disagree
> • An audience to listen to the debate and decide the outcome by voting

3 The introducer starts the debate by introducing the topic, for example, 'Today we are debating whether or not a skateboard ramp should be built on the playground'.

4 The introducer then invites the team who agree with the topic to put forward their views.

5 After listening to their arguments, the opposition are invited to speak.

6 Finally the audience votes on which side has won by being the most persuasive.

Using talk to debate

Both sides can use persuasive tricks. There are also some special words and phrases that are useful when putting forward a viewpoint.

The team that agrees

The team that disagrees

We believe...

It is true that...

Our first reason is...

Also...

The main reason to vote for us is that...

Furthermore...

Another reason for saying this...

Finally...

On the other hand...

It is not right to say... because...

If...

The other team is incorrect to suggest... because...

However...

Other people suggest that...

A different view is to suggest that...

Alternatively...

Finally, the most important reason for voting for us is...

Debating tricks

When you are debating remember these key points
about talking to your audience.

- Speak loudly and clearly so everyone can hear you.
- Look at the audience – scan the room to take in
  everyone.
- Use gestures to support what you say.
- Try to appear reasonable and friendly.
- Appeal to the feelings of the audience ('how would
  you feel if...').
- Keep to the time allowed.

Debating rules

There are only a few rules for a debate. Usually the
introducer makes sure that both teams keep to the rules.

1 Take turns to speak: only one team can speak at a time.
2 The audience must listen.
3 Allow a minute's thinking time before the audience votes.

Attention grabbers

Here are some ideas for grabbing attention.

- A dramatic photo to back up a point.
- A poem or song to emphasize a point.
- Someone talking about a real experience.
- A list of facts.
- A tape of someone speaking in favour.
- A video clip of someone famous who supports their view.
- An object that demonstrates something.
- Using humour to destroy an argument.
- Ending on three key points.

Ideas for debates

Should we eat kangaroo meat?
Should smoking be banned in public places?
Should you be able to buy better food in schools?
School uniform – should it be banned?
Should medicines be tested on animals?
Should mobile phones be allowed in school?
Should children be allowed to use chat rooms on the Internet?
Should children have to stay at school at the end of the day to do an hour of homework?

4
Drama games

Are you an avid TV watcher? Do you suffer from square eyes? If so, you like drama! Here are some good drama games to get you into a creative mood.

Good morning, Your Majesty

Choose someone to be king or queen and sit on the throne blindfolded. The person in charge points at someone who goes to the throne and says, 'Good morning, Your Majesty' in a disguised voice. The king or queen has to guess who it is. If the guess is wrong the new person becomes king or queen. The winner is the person with the most correct guesses.

Home

Play this in teams. The aim is for one player to move from one end of a hall to the other without being touched. The team trying to stop the player is blindfolded. They listen carefully to hear the player creeping up the hall and then touch them.

Phoning home

Work in pairs, sitting back to back. One person picks up an imaginary phone and rings the other. They then hold a conversation. This works well if the person phoning pretends to be a character from a story the class is reading, for example, Alex Rider ringing a friend during one of his adventures.

The button game

You need a collection of odd buttons for this. Someone selects a button and then tells everyone the story behind the button, using the following questions:

- What piece of clothing did it come from?
- Who was wearing it?
- Where were they when it dropped off?
- How did it come off?
- What was the wearer doing?
- Where was the wearer going?
- What happened when they reached their destination?

Mime it!

Everyone sits in a circle with a box in the middle. Someone comes into the centre and mimes taking something out of the box and using it. They could choose:

an object	something to eat	a toy
a gadget	a piece of clothing	a machine
an animal	something to do with a game or sport	

After 30 seconds, the person freezes and everyone tries to guess what was in the box.

Crazy excuses

You are late for school. Stand up and give a crazy excuse, telling the others the story of what happened.

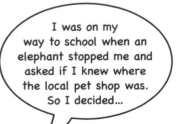

I was on my way to school when an elephant stopped me and asked if I knew where the local pet shop was. So I decided...

Monologues and duologues

A monologue is a speech given by a character; in a duologue two characters are talking. They can be great fun.

Preparing a monologue

Draw an outline of a character on a large sheet of paper. Then write and draw what you know about the character, what they look like, etc. Add what they might be thinking or feeling, using speech or thought bubbles. If you are reading a class story you could add extra information, lists of likes and dislikes, key events, and quotes as you discover more about the character.

In a monologue, you play the role of the chosen character. You talk aloud and reveal the thoughts in the head of your character – this might mean showing your feelings, going over what has happened and worrying about what will happen. You might be about to reveal your plans or your motives for what you have done. Remember to start with 'I' – because you are in the role of someone else talking aloud, e.g. 'I was a bit scared when the peach began to move but now I've got used to it…'

Have a go and see what you come up with. It helps to use a tape-recorder. Use this simple pattern to help you structure what you talk about.

What happened.

    How you felt about it.

        What you think of others involved.

            What you think will happen next.

            How you feel about that.

                What you are going to do now.

Keep practising the monologue – it may only last a minute or two at the most. You will find that if you repeat it often enough you will soon know every word. This is helpful if you are going to perform it for your class.

Before you perform the monologue think about:

> • Do you need a costume?
> • Should you sit or stand?
> • Do you need any props?
> • Should you move at all?
> • What sort of expressions should you have?

Remember to keep your voice clear and loud enough to be heard and to use expression to show what the character is feeling.

Preparing a duologue

Duologues are good fun because you work in pairs. They are usually quite short – up to about three minutes. In a duologue you both act out a scene. Begin by thinking about the two different characters you will play. What sort of people are you? How do you feel about each other? Try choosing a feeling from the list below – something different for each character. Also discuss why your character is feeling like that.

angry	**sad**	**lonely**	**worried**
excited	**happy**	**jealous**	**mean**
left out	**clumsy**	**picked on**	**curious**
adventurous	**shy**	**chatty**	**afraid**
confident	**cruel**	**clumsy**	**giggly**

Talk about something in role. Remember how your character is feeling – will this make them say and do different things?

Stay in role. If your character is angry you stay angry, saying cross things and being grumpy. You can't suddenly cheer up – unless something happens to cheer you up.

Next you need an event to build your duologue around. Here are a few ideas. Choose one and act it out, making it up as you go along. Keep rehearsing and in the end you will know your lines and be ready to present the duologue to others.

Ideas for duologues

Waiting for a late bus – one of you is in a rush.
One wants to go into a deserted house; the other one doesn't.
Meeting the day after breaking up as friends.
Asking Mum for more pocket money.
One wants to go to the cinema; the other to the park.
Explain to Gran how you broke a favourite bowl.

Improvising

Improvisation is fun because you make up what to say and do as you go along. You could think of life as one enormous improvisation – because we are all constantly making up what to say next and deciding how to behave.

Work in small groups and try improvising these scenarios.
- Everyone has done really well in a test except one of you.
- You are late home and have missed seeing Auntie Doreen.
- You have torn the new jeans your mum bought.
- Sitting on a bench next to a child whose balloon has burst.
- Stealing a packet of crisps and being caught by Dad.
- You are a magician who has lost his rabbit.
- You are an alien who joins a bus queue.

The tiger game

Next try a scene in which three of you are sitting in a café. A tiger walks in. It has escaped from the zoo. Take it in turns to be the tiger, and make the tiger different each time, e.g.
- it wants to return to the zoo because the food was good;
- it misses India;
- it wants a job in films;
- it wants to become a vegetarian but no one will believe it.

Things to avoid

having a fight   being silly
going over the top   exaggerating too much
coming out of role   laughing

Using cards

Start by preparing a pile of small cards. You will need a set of character cards (a princess, a cat, a giant, a witch, etc) and a set of place cards (marketplace, bus queue, classroom, kitchen, forest, spaceship, etc). Finally you need a set of triggers: small, dramatic events that start the improvisation.

> you hear a scream   the phone rings
> there is a knock at the door   a letter arrives
> the electricity goes off   a dog barks

Shuffle the cards and put them in three piles. The players choose a character card and a place card which tells them where they meet. Why are they there, what are they are doing and what will they do next? Finally, they choose a trigger card.

The players begin improvising at a signal. After three minutes they freeze on a second signal and another group chooses cards and improvises. People watching try to work out who each person is, where they are and what the trigger was.

Fairy-tale games

Traditional tales make great games. Here are a few ideas.
• Conduct interviews, e.g. the troll from under the bridge.
• Read the six o'clock news, including headlines about the destruction of houses belonging to local pigs.
• Hold a conversation between Mrs Wolf and her husband, who is out of breath, huffing and puffing all the time.
• Stage a trial, e.g. put Goldilocks or the wolf on trial for house breaking.

Writing a play

Another great drama idea is to write and put on a play. First of all think about your audience – this will help you decide what sort of play and storyline might be suitable.

A simple way to plan a play is to use a flow chart with a box for each scene. Try to have just a few scenes. This flow chart shows a simple outline for the start of a play called *The King's Toymakers*. You could finish it by adding more scenes and then writing the speeches and a few stage directions.

Scene 1 Proclamation: the king wants all toymakers to come to the palace.

Scene 2 Jim, a very poor toymaker, leaves home, bidding his family farewell.

Scene 3 Jim arrives at the palace with lots of other toymakers. The king asks them to build a toy for his child's birthday. Jim carves a beautiful doll – but just as he finishes he discovers that the king's child is a boy.

How to write a play

The key point is that you only write down what the characters say. You can give a few stage directions to tell the actors what to do, where to go or how to say something. But don't use too many. Write the name of the character speaking on the left hand side and leave a space before writing what they say. Don't worry about using speech marks!

Remember to keep the characters in role – if Jim is unhappy, then make sure he keeps making gloomy remarks until something happens to make him happier. Begin each scene by saying where the characters are and adding any important details. Here is the opening of the second scene.

Scene 2

Jim, a toymaker, is at home in the kitchen. His wife, Mary, is serving their six children (Abel, Jenny, Saul, Peter, Sam, Jim Junior). They are all poorly dressed.

Jim   It's not soup again is it?

Mary   I'm sorry Jim, but it's all we can afford.

Jenny   *(whining)* This is just water – there's nothing in it.

Mary   Don't make a fuss Jenny – here, have some of mine. There is some rice in the bottom.

Jim is packing a sack with his tools.

Mary   What are you up to?

Jim   The king is looking for a toymaker. It's a great chance. I expect every toymaker in the land will be going.

Mary   Well, you had better set out for the palace straight away because this could mean we make our fortune…

Putting on your play

Here are some top tips for putting on a play.

Rehearse

You need to rehearse a lot so everyone knows their lines and can act their part. It helps to video your performance so you can all see how you could improve. One person should act as the director and check that the audience can hear the lines and see what is happening.

Learn your lines

It won't be much of a play if the actors forget their lines! Here are some ways to remember your lines.
• Record the lines on a tape and listen to it often.
• Test each other in pairs.
• Write out your lines.
• Write tricky lines in colour to make them stand out.
• Write lines on small cards and carry them with you.

Speak loudly enough

Ask the director to stand at the back of the hall to check that everyone can be heard easily. Everyone should practise saying their lines loudly and clearly.

Watch the speed

Try not to rush your lines during the performance. If people gabble no one will be able to work out what they are saying, or what's happening in the play.

Use expression

Think about what the lines mean and change your voice so you say them with expression. Try to make sure that if you are saying something cross then you sound angry. Try saying your lines in different ways to see which sounds most effective.

Beware of blocking

It is important not to stand in front of each other on stage. This is called blocking. If you stand in front of someone else then the audience will not be able to hear or see them acting!

Face the audience

If you stand with your back to the audience no one will be able to hear what you are saying. Make sure that when you are speaking you face the audience.

Have costumes and props

Dressing up helps you to feel like someone else. You may have to find items for your costume at home. You will probably need props for your play, too. These are objects which can help to make the play seem more realistic, and they can include furniture.

Move in character

When you are moving about on the stage try to stay in role. Think about how your character feels and then move accordingly. For instance, if your character is supposed to be angry then you need to stomp across the stage to show the audience how you feel.

5
Journalists at large

Interviewing is a great way to find out information about any topic you might be studying in school.

Interview skills

Practise interviewing skills. One key skill is to think about the type of question to ask. To find out specific information you need to ask closed questions, e.g. 'What colour is custard?' This is a closed question because there is nothing else to add. These questions are useful when you need simple answers.

If you want the person being interviewed to talk about something that has happened, what they know, or how they do something, ask open questions. Chat show hosts use them when they want someone to talk for a while. If you ask, 'Can you tell us about how you became famous?' you expect quite a long answer. That is an open question.

Practise asking open and closed questions by interviewing each other. You could pretend that you are about to interview a famous person because you are writing their biography. Make a list of five closed questions (e.g. Where were you born?) and five open questions. Then interview each other.

In the hot seat

One of you sits in the hot seat and plays someone else.
Everyone questions the person in the hot seat, who could be:

- a character from a story, e.g. Harry Potter
- a famous person from history, Henry VIII
- an ordinary person from history, e.g. a chimney sweep

List questions designed to find out what you want to know.
Be clear about why you are questioning the person and what
you want to know. Hot seating works best when the person
in the hot seat knows a lot about the character and answers
questions about thoughts, feelings and motives.

Professor Know-it-all

Work in pairs. One plays a TV reporter interviewing the
world expert Professor Know-it-all about a topic – this could
be something you are studying in history, geography, science….
The reporter uses a phrase such as 'Tell me about…' to
start the professor talking. The skill lies in encouraging the
interviewee to talk. You could say:

- Tell me more about…
- What happened when…?
- I am interested in…
- Can you tell us how…?
- What thoughts do you have about…?

Just a minute

In this game everyone writes down a question about a topic
on a slip of paper. These are put into a hat. Then everyone
chooses a different slip (not their own). The challenge is to
talk for one minute about the topic. The winner is the person
who manages to speak for one minute without hesitating or
wandering off the subject.

Television broadcasts

These are great fun. Everyone has watched the news on TV. An 'anchor' in the studio announces the news:

Good evening. This is the six o'clock news from Class 6. A giant peach has been seen flying over the Atlantic Ocean...

Often, the anchor talks to someone in an outside broadcast unit, e.g. a reporter who interviews witnesses. 'Hello Jeremy. I'm on the deck of *HMS Catcher*. I have with me Captain Justseenit who saw the peach. Captain, what can you tell us about it?'

In class, work in small groups and rehearse the broadcast. You could build it around a story you know well, for instance, the poem 'The Highwayman' by Alfred Noyes. The reporter might interview a soldier or the landlord about what has happened. Another idea is to interview a character from a story, for example, one of Jack's neighbours about the beanstalk that grew overnight and how the family are suddenly wealthy.

Alien landing

This idea works well if you have a means of recording your performance. Create a short news programme about an alien sighting. You need an anchor person – the main newsreader – and TV journalists, who conduct interviews with:
• someone who heard something odd;
• someone who saw the spacecraft;
• someone who claims to have been abducted;
• an expert in aliens;
• a police officer called to the site.

You need someone who can hold the video camera still enough to capture the events. Work out the sequence.

Signature tune of the beginning of the TV news, plus board saying Six o'clock News

Anchor person introduces the headlines – alien abduction reported from...
hands over to outside broadcast unit

Interview 1
a dog walker who heard something

Interview 2
someone who saw the craft

Interview 3
someone who claims to have been abducted previously

Interview 4
policeman

Back to studio
for anchor to interview expert in aliens

End of news complete with image of spaceship in sky and headline ALIENS LANDING

The broadcast will need rehearsing to make sure that the interviews sound realistic. The people being interviewed need to think about what happened to them:
• what they were doing;
• where they were going;
• what they saw or heard;
• how they reacted;
• how they feel now.
The reporters need to have their questions ready.

Think about about the language you use.
Try comparing a news broadcast with a programme on children's television – which is more formal and why?

Props

Music to start and end news
Board with headlines
Pictures of sky with spaceship image
Clipboards and microphones
Desk for anchor plus two chairs

6
Storytelling

**Storytelling is magic. You can lie in bed and be
transported into another world, or sit in a cinema
and enter the world of a film. Stories come in many
forms. Think of them as branches of a story tree.**

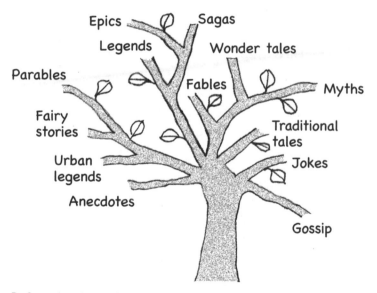

Epics Sagas
Legends Wonder tales
Parables Fables Myths
Fairy stories Traditional tales
Urban legends Jokes
Anecdotes Gossip

Before the days of books and TV, everyone told stories. There
are thousands of traditional tales across the world that started
by being told. They were often told by storytellers who
travelled from village to village telling tales in exchange for food
and a bed for the night. You may have seen a storyteller in
school. Here's how to become one yourself.

Choosing a story to tell

Look through collections of traditional tales and find a story you like which is short and simple. The easiest to tell are those you know already, such as 'The Billy Goats Gruff'. Starting with something simple gives you confidence. The more stories you learn, the easier it becomes.

Preparing to tell a story

Storytellers have different ways of remembering stories. Which one suits you?

1 Story picture maps

Draw a story picture map – pictures of the characters and events. You can add words to act as prompts. Drawing the map helps to visualize the story (see it in your mind). You can see the whole plot in one place on the page.

2 Storyboard

Try drawing a cartoon version of the main events.
This is called a storyboard. Stick to the key events.

| *Little goat ...* | *... meets troll on bridge ...* | *... is allowed to cross ...* | *... bigger goat ...* |

| *... meets troll on bridge ...* | *... is allowed to cross ...* | *... biggest goat meets troll ...* | *... and tosses him into river.* |

3 The story's skeleton

Some people work out the bare bones of a story. What are
the main incidents? Try to end up with five or six. Write them
in boxes in a flow chart with prompt words. Then write the
prompt words on separate cards to help recall the sequence.

Little goat trots over bridge

Troll stops him

Little goat says wait for bigger brother

Repeat twice

Big goat knocks troll into river

4 Act it

Another idea is to put a few simple actions to the story. These movements help you remember what is happening and they also help the listener understand. So you might use your hands or face to convey chopping, cutting, picking up, smiling and so on. Keep the actions simple and do not have too many.

5 Use a tape

Making a recording of the story can help. Remember to leave spaces between each sentence. Then replay the tape over and over again, repeating each sentence in the space. This is a good way to learn a story if you learn best through listening.

6 Practise

Keep retelling the story to yourself. You may feel daft standing in your room or walking down the road muttering the story aloud, but it does help. After a while you will remember a version of it. It doesn't matter if the words change a bit each time you tell it. That is all part of being a storyteller. It helps if you have a friend who will listen!

7 Story partners and circles

Try working in pairs and retell the story a few times, till you are both really good at it. There are two ways to do this.
• You can both tell the story at the same time as though you are looking into a mirror.
• You can take it in turns – with the listener helping the teller. Story circles are fun. You sit in a circle and retell the story, taking turns at saying the next sentence or event.

Telling the tale

Now you are ready, but you need an audience!
For a fairy tale find some younger children. Start by
telling it to a small group. Once you are confident, try
telling it to larger numbers. You could tell the story in pairs,
helping each other – and when you are confident, go solo!

Points to remember

- Make sure your audience is comfortable and
looking at you.
- Do not rush the telling – vary the pace. For
instance you might want to speed up a little in
a chase. Some places may need dramatic pauses.
- Make sure that the words are clear and can be
heard. Can everyone hear?
- Use expression – make the troll sound angry
or frightening. Make the little billy goat sound
terrified and timid.
- Lean forward as you tell the tale and use your
eyes. Look at the audience and into their eyes
as you tell the tale. Scan the group and hold
their attention with your eyes. Make your eyes
larger by opening them wide!
- If you are telling a tale to younger children and
you see that they are becoming frightened you
say something like, 'but the little goat was not
afraid'. Good storytellers adapt the story for
their audience.

Changing tales

Once you know a story really well, you can make it your own. This can be done by changing it in various ways.

- Change the names and places. You could have a story about the three bold bison and instead of a troll you might have a wolf under the bridge.
- Add extra description or events. So you might have a section in which the troll makes an elaborate trap for the big goat which is then broken.
- Alter the characters, setting or events. Instead of Goldilocks and three bears you might have secret agent called Gold E. Locks who breaks into the headquarters of a gang of robbers, led by the infamous Mister Big.
- Retell the tale from a different angle. You could have a wolf telling the story of how he saw a tornado approaching the pig's house and tried to save the poor fellow!
- Use the plot with different characters. Instead of the Billy Goats Gruff, you might have three snowmen who want to cross the road and sneak into a freezer to snowbathe!

Easy stories to begin with

The Billy Goats Gruff	The Gingerbread Man
The Little Red Hen	The Magic Porridge Pot
The Enormous Turnip	Rumplestiltskin
The Three Pigs	Red Riding Hood
The Three Bears	Jack and the Beanstalk
Stone Soup	Cinderella.

How well did I do?

Try this quiz to check your speaking and listening skills. Write down the answer which applies best to you.

Part One: Speaking

1 When I give a talk, people:
a) Often ask me to repeat what I've said.
b) Look at me and listen with interest.
c) Mostly don't listen, but fool around, pass notes and chat.

2 If I was speaking in an assembly, I would:
a) Tell my grandad's corny jokes to relax everyone and get them groaning.
b) Do a lot of preparation and practice to make sure my talk is the right length and level for the people I'm talking to.
c) Get the book with the most information on the subject out of the library and read from it for half an hour.

3 During a talk, I:
a) Screw up my eyes so I won't see my best mate and forget what I was going to say.
b) Scan the audience to make sure they know I am talking to all of them.
c) Freeze and fix my eyes on the back wall the whole time.

4 While I am speaking, I:
a) Keep my face rigid in case I crack up laughing.
b) Use facial expressions to reinforce what I am saying.
c) Try not to let my face twitch because I'm nervous.

5 When I respond to something someone has said, I:
a) Say the first thing that comes into my head.
b) Take a moment to think about my answer before speaking.
c) Take so long to organize my thoughts that sometimes
   I don't get to speak at all.

6 When someone argues against me, I:
a) Make sure I shout louder than them so I drown them out.
b) Think about what they say and whether it affects my views.
c) Put my hands over my ears so I can't be affected by what
   they think.

7 When I'm taking part in a debate, I:
a) Always interrupt if I don't agree with what someone's saying.
b) Hear people out before responding to their points.
c) Don't like to say anything in case it offends someone.

8 When I have to give a presentation, I:
a) Have a quick look on my mum's Internet before school.
b) Make a note of the key points I want to make on postcards.
c) Get so nervous that I say the first thing that comes into my
   head and hope that it will be over soon.

Mostly As: Your approach is self-centred and too laid
back – take a long hard look at your style, prepare your
presentations and listen to other people's point of view.

Mostly Bs: Congratulations – you seem to be taking the
right approach – when's your next presentation?

Mostly Cs: You need to try speaking up for yourself and your
beliefs – with the right preparation you can do it and enjoy it.

Part Two: Listening

9 When someone else is talking, I:
a) Get out my mini joke book and try a few on my mates.
b) Go off into my favourite daydream.
c) Listen, look at the speaker, smile and respond.

10 When a speaker gives us lots of information, I:
a) Get bored and have a game of thumb war with my mate.
b) Decide I'll never be able to remember it all and stop listening.
c) Clarify what they've said by recapping and asking questions.

11 When a speaker has finished a presentation, I:
a) Check my watch and count down to when the bell goes.
b) Try not to attract attention in case I'm asked a question.
c) Recall the main ideas and reply to what has been said.

12 At the end of a talk, I:
a) Ask if they'd like to hear a few of my favourite jokes.
b) Wonder aloud what's for lunch.
c) Ask questions about the topic.

Mostly As: Calm down and start listening – there're loads of fascinating things out there just waiting to be discovered – don't miss them.

Mostly Bs: Wake up and start listening – you'll learn loads and will soon start to feel more confident.

Mostly Cs: You listen well and respond appropriately – well done!

Glossary

adapt To change or alter for a purpose, e.g. to change how you speak when you are in different situations.

alliteration Starting words with the same sound.

audience People who are listening.

chairperson Someone chosen to run a group.

debate Two sides putting forwards their viewpoints, usually with an audience listening, who then decides what they think.

duologue A short scene with only two characters talking.

expression Changing how you say something to show your feelings, e.g. speaking in an angry voice.

hot seating Someone pretending to be a character and being interviewed by the rest of the class.

imperatives A command, usually starting with a bossy verb that tells you what to do, e.g. Run to the end of the playground.

improvising Making up something on the spur of the moment.

interviewing Asking someone questions.

mentor A group member who helps to complete a task, making sure everyone has spoken and checking that everyone agrees.

mime To pretend to do something using actions, not speech.

monologue A character talking aloud on their own, usually about their thoughts, feelings and what is happening.

newsreader A person on TV who reads the news.

pace The speed at which you talk.

persuasive language Using words to try to make someone believe what you are saying.

plot The main sequence of events in a story.

reporter A person whose job it is to find out news and report it for radio, TV or a newspaper.

role play Making up a scene in which everyone takes on a different role and pretends to be someone else.

scribe A person in a group who writes down the main points.

setting The place where a story happens.

storyboard A cartoon version of a story that shows the main events.

Index